"Man's heart away from
nature becomes hard."

~ *Standing Bear*

Cover Design by Michael Arnott

Special thanks to Naturalist Tim Irvin for contributing his expertise on the wildlife of the Great Bear Rainforest.

Printed in Canada by Friesens

Library and Archives Canada Cataloguing in Publication

Harrington, Jennifer, 1973-, author
    Spirit bear / by Jennifer Harrington ; illustrated by Michael Arnott.

Issued in print and electronic formats.
ISBN 978-0-9920320-0-5 (pbk.).--ISBN 978-0-9920320-1-2 (epub).--ISBN 978-0-9920320-2-9 (animated epub)

    1. Bears--Juvenile fiction. I. Arnott, Michael, 1973-, illustrator II. Title.

PS8615.A7472S65 2013   jC813'.6   C2013-905375-1
                                        C2013-905376-X

SPIRIT BEAR

by Jennifer Harrington

Illustrated by Michael Arnott

www.ecobooks4kids.com

On a cold, dark winter's night, deep in the Great Bear Rainforest, a little baby bear cub named Annuk was born.

He was tiny and blind, with no fur at all. Next to him were two more cubs, a brother and a sister.

Outside in the forest, the wind howled and the icy rain beat down, but in their cozy den beneath an old cedar tree, the bears were safe and warm.

The cubs nuzzled close to Mama to nurse, and there they stayed all winter long, underground.

When spring came, Mama led the cubs out of the dark den into the bright, lush, green rainforest.

They had grown very big all winter on Mama's milk, and they had thick fur from head to toe.

Mama took them exploring in the forest, where they snacked on sedges, munched on skunk cabbage, dined on berries and gobbled insects.

The cubs loved play-fighting, and they'd wrestle every day, tumbling together on the forest floor.

Life was good in the Great Bear Rainforest.

One day, while drinking from a little brook, Annuk caught sight of his reflection in the water.

For the very first time, he saw that he looked different from his family. He wasn't black at all.

He was pure WHITE from head to toe!!!

"Why do I look different, Mama?" he asked.

"Your white fur makes you special, Annuk," she said. "One day you will catch more salmon than any bear in the forest. You are a spirit bear."

This made Annuk feel very proud, and he thought it must be quite a good thing to be a spirit bear.

When autumn came, it was time to learn to fish!

Mama took the cubs to the river where they watched the salmon LEAP right out of the water, into Mama's waiting teeth and claws!

Annuk was excited. He knew spirit bears were good at catching salmon, so he wanted to try to catch one for himself.

When he saw a really BIG salmon swim by, he JUMPED into the river and caught it in his teeth.

But as he landed, he SLIPPED and fell into the water! The river was high and the current was strong, but Annuk refused to let go of his salmon.

He tried with all of his might to swim to shore, but the raging river swept Annuk and his salmon downstream, far away from his family.

After a little while, the river began to slow, and Annuk climbed to shore. He was very tired, so he lay down and fell asleep next to his salmon.

But when he woke up, his salmon was missing... A little sea wolf cub was dragging it into the woods!

"STOP THIEF!" he cried. He ran up and snatched his salmon back, and the little sea wolf ran off. Annuk began to eat. He ate and ate and ate.

But it was too big to finish. The little wolf was still watching him from the woods, so he decided to share. Annuk backed away from his salmon.

The wolf ran up and began to eat. She ate and ate and ate. Then she disappeared into the forest.

Annuk was alone, he was lost, and he was on the wrong side of the river. But he refused to give up.

Suddenly a bald eagle SWOOPED down out of the sky and snatched up the rest of his salmon.

"I'm lost!" Annuk said to the eagle.
"Do you know where I can cross the river?"

"AWWKK!" said the eagle, and flew off with his fish.

"KER-SPLASH!" Annuk saw a whale breaching out in the water. "I'm lost!" Annuk called out to him.
"Do you know where I can cross the river?"

"WHHHHOOOOAAAANNNN!!!" said the whale, and he swam away. Annuk sighed.

He began to walk up the riverbank all alone.
But someone was following him...

Suddenly Annuk heard a low GROWL behind him. He turned and saw a dark, vicious little creature with sharp teeth, sharp claws and flashing eyes!

"I'm lost!" Annuk said nervously to the creature. "Do you know where I can cross the river?"

"Are you lost, little bear?" The young wolverine hissed. "I think I'll have you for my lunch!"

"My pack will hunt you down and eat you up if you touch that bear!" cried a voice from above.

It was the wolf cub, growling and baring her teeth!

The wolverine gnashed her teeth and scratched her claws on the log. She snapped her jaws angrily.

"Lucky for you, I don't like the taste of bears," she growled, and ran off into the forest.

"If that wolverine was older, she'd have had us for lunch!" said the wolf. "My name is Kaya."

"I'm Annuk," he said. "Thank you for saving me! I'm lost. Do you know where I can cross the river?"

"Yes I do! I'll take you there." Suddenly she froze, and then she disappeared inside a hollow log. "In here!" Kaya whispered. So Annuk followed her.

"CRUNCH CRUNCH!" A huge animal was coming. Annuk peered through a crack in the log, and saw a giant claw, flashing eyes and BIG sharp teeth!

The grizzly bear gnashed his teeth and scratched his claws on the log. He snapped his jaws angrily.

"Lucky for you, I just ate a big salmon" the grizzly bear growled, and lumbered off into the woods.

"Let's keep moving," Kaya said, once the grizzly was gone. "There are predators everywhere!"

They walked for a while, but something was wrong. "We're being stalked," Kaya whispered.

High on a rocky ledge across the river, a cougar was crouched, tail twitching, ready to pounce! She had sharp teeth, sharp claws and glowing green eyes. She growled HUNGRILY at them.

"Lucky for you, the river is high, and I hate water!" she snarled. "Or else you two would be my supper!"

The cat gnashed her teeth and scratched her claws on the rocks. She snapped her jaws angrily.

"Yikes!" cried Annuk, "Let's get out of here!!!"

They ran as fast as they could up the riverbank until the cougar was out of sight.

"We are nearly at the river crossing. I'll have to turn back once we get there," Kaya said.

As they stopped for a drink of water at the river's edge, they heard a strange sound from the opposite bank: "Moksgm'ol, Mosksgm'ol!"

On the far shore, two strange, dark-skinned creatures were standing up on their hind legs, and pointing right at Annuk!

"I don't think they want to hurt us," Kaya said. "I think they just like your white fur."

Annuk smiled, and let the creatures watch him for a moment, and then they carried on up the river.

At last they came to the river crossing, and Annuk set out across the long, slippery, mossy log.

Halfway across he slipped and fell, and his legs swung out over the river! "ANNUK!" Kaya shouted.

"LOOK OUT! LOOK OUT!" squealed an otter who was feasting on a salmon down below.

Annuk took a deep breath. He refused to give up. He dug his claws in and pulled himself up with all of his might. Then he carefully inched all the way across to the opposite side of the river.

"I made it! I made it!" he shouted.

"You did it! Don't give up Annuk, I know you'll find your way home!" Kaya shouted back.

"I couldn't have made it this far without you, Kaya, thank you so much!" he called to her.

"Any time, my friend!" she replied, and then she turned and disappeared into the forest.

Annuk was alone again. His friend was gone. He was still lost, and night was beginning to fall.

A chill ran down his spine as the sky grew dark. Suddenly, Annuk heard something following him, so he began to RUN!!!

He heard a growl as he climbed up a nearby snag, and he felt hot breath on his back.

He looked down to see a BIG black wolf, with sharp teeth, sharp claws and flashing yellow eyes!

"All alone, little bear? I can wait for you all night, and have you for my breakfast!" he snarled.

"BEWARE! BEWARE!" croaked a raven sitting on a branch next to him in the dead tree.

Annuk shivered in the dark. There was no escape.

All night the wolf circled the snag, gnashing his teeth and scratching his claws on the ground.

Annuk refused to give up. There must be SOME way to distract the wolf so that he could escape! Then he spotted a large wolverine slinking around in the trees, and suddenly he had an idea.

"Haallooo, you there!" Annuk called to him. "Hungry this morning? Wouldn't you love to EAT me up?"

"Oh yes," hissed the wolverine, "I think I'd enjoy that!"

"Oh no you don't!" growled the wolf. "That little white bear cub is going to be MY breakfast!"

He lunged right at the wolverine, who hissed and snarled, and soon they were twisting together in a wild, frightening frenzy of fur and fangs.

As the two animals fought, Annuk quietly climbed down from the snag and ran off into the forest.

Annuk ran as fast as he could towards the den where he was born. He was tired and weak, but he refused to give up. He had come so far!

He came to a grassy field and saw three black bears on the opposite side. "Mama!" he shouted.

"Annuk! You're ALIVE!!!" his Mama cried out.

The bears ran to the middle of the field where they tumbled and rolled together in the long grass. "We missed you so much!" cried his sister. "We thought you'd drowned!" cried his brother.

"No," said Annuk, "I'm alive! I was lost and afraid, but I never gave up. And I made it! I made it home!"

His mother smiled warmly at her long-lost cub. "Welcome home, my brave little spirit bear!"

The End